You're a Good Sport, Miss Malarkey

First published in the United States of America in 2002
by Walker Publishing Company, Inc.

Published simultaneously in Canada by Fitzhenry and Whiteside,
Markham, Ontario L3R 4T8

For information about permission to reproduce selections from
this book, write to Permissions, Walker & Company, 435 Hudson Street,
New York, New York 10014

Library of Congress Cataloging-in-Publication Data
Finchler, Judy.
  You're a good sport, Miss Malarkey / Judy Finchler and Kevin
O'Malley.
    p. cm.
  Summary: The children on a newly formed soccer team love their
coach, Miss Malarkey, who doesn't know much about the game except how
to make it fun, but the school principal and parents have other ideas.
  ISBN 0-8027-8815-7 — ISBN 0-8027-8816-5 (lib. bdg.)
  [1. Soccer—Fiction. 2. Sportsmanship—Fiction.
3. Coaching (Athletics)—Fiction.]
I. O'Malley, Kevin, 1961-ill. II. Title.

PZ7.F4956658 Yo 2002
[Fic]—dc21   2002023063

The illustrations for this book were created in watercolor and
colored pencil on 140-pound watercolor paper.

Book design by Sophie Ye Chin

Calligraphy by Martha Myers

Printed in Hong Kong

2 4 6 8 10 9 7 5 3 1

To my sister,
Ellen Decker,
school principal
extraordinaire,
and the growing
Decker family.
—J. F.

STAFF MEETING
Union issues and 'THE TEST'
Many of our members have
expressd discomfort with the
current events in education.
Union Rep. D. Manda Ourshara
will be on hand to discuss
the union position.
**FRIDAY NIGHT
AT UNION HALL**

**SOCCER
SIGN-UPS**

SEPT. 8

You can't win, if you don't play
So sign up today!!!!!!!!!!!

PTA MEETING

How to apply for
and win college scholarship
money for your elementary -
aged child.

**PRESENTED BY:
Dr. I. Intendtoscareia**
The doctor has helped
thousands of parents get the
kind of headstart that

SCORES On the l
state-wide test.

MATH
ENGLISH
GYM
MUSIC
ART

The state will be elim
the art portion of the
next year

You're a Good Sport, Miss Malarkey

Judy Finchler
and
Kevin O'Malley

Walker & Company
New York

NOAH

Wonc there
A Turky name
Bob.
He koud drive
d car
        The End
        Ryan Scott

CONNOR

A Turkey Was
Watching TV
When his stepd
brother took
the REmote
        Quinn

DARA

Since our minds are in good shape from all the learning and tests in school, our principal, Mr. Wiggins, says it's time to work on being fit. We're not just part of a school, now we're part of a soccer league. It's called YELS (Youngstown Elementary League Soccer).

Mr. Wiggins was our first coach.

He showed us how to head the ball.

But he had problems.

Mr. Fitanuff, our gym teacher, took over for him. Then at practice one day he was explaining the best way to corner kick.

But nobody could understand what he was saying.

WINNING Corner KICKS

YOU →
GOAL →
BALL →

So now Miss Malarkey is our coach. Mr. Wiggins always says she's a team player. She's real nice, but she says she doesn't know that much about soccer. That's okay with me. Most of the kids on our team have never played soccer before anyway.

Everybody has their own talents, says Miss Malarkey.
Sean runs really fast. He runs around and around and around.

Lauren can really kick the ball. She kicks it all over the place.

Patrick is really funny. He makes everyone laugh.

And Jason should have his own team. He dribbles really well.

We usually have a big crowd at our games. Most of the parents are there. Brothers and sisters get to watch too. Whenever grandparents come, they always get treated the best.

Katelyn's dad always comes late. Maya's dad and Justin's mom have phones attached to their ears. Sean's dad always worries about everyone on the team. And Tyler's mom is cool 'cause she brings snacks.

We have a lot of fun at practice.
Miss Malarkey is a fun coach.
We practice kicking the ball.

And how *not* to use our hands.

We play follow the leader.

But we still haven't won any games. So I guess the parents are trying to help us, but they don't seem to be having much fun. They're always yelling.

COME ON... HUSTLE!

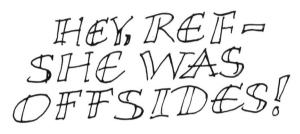

HEY, REF— SHE WAS OFFSIDES!

PASS THE BALL, SHORTY!

On Friday Miss Malarkey called a team meeting. She told us how much better we've gotten. She said she was proud of us. And she said that at Saturday's game she wanted us to try our best.

Principal Wiggins called our team into his office the same day. He told us how important it is to win. Saturday's big game is against East Braggerly Elementary. "We have to beat Principal Wretchet . . . I mean . . . it's important to try your hardest to beat these guys."

Saturday's game started off really well. Everybody tried and nobody cried when they fell down or made a bad mistake. It was fun, but it was pretty weird because the parents were sort of quiet. They looked sort of nervous.

The trouble started after halftime when the other team scored a goal.

Principal Wiggins ran over to suggest a few plays.
Melissa's mom told Miss Malarkey that Melissa wasn't playing enough.

Jason's father started yelling for everybody to hustle. Sean's mom
said Jason was a ball hog. So Jason's mom started yelling at her.

By not putting my daughter in the game, you are inflicting possible long-term developmental damage on her athletic growth... she'll never get a sports scholarship.

The other team kicked the ball and it hit Jimmy and he fell down.
His parents ran onto the field and the referee called for a penalty shot.

That's when Sean's dad and Principal Wiggins ran onto the field. The other team's parents started yelling. Three babies and a grandpa who were napping woke up and started to cry. I mean, only the babies started to cry, not the grandpa.

Everybody was going nuts.
Miss Malarkey threw her soccer book into the air and yelled—

They sort of had to cancel that game.

Things are different now. They changed the name of the league and everything. Instead of YELS it's now called SILENT (Soccer Instructional League, Elementary Neighborhood Teams). Parents aren't allowed to yell or cheer. They can only clap really politely.

All the parents are given lollipops before the games to help keep them from yelling.

Miss Malarkey is still our coach. She's really nice, and she hardly ever has to use her soccer book anymore.

Sometimes she still yells, though. She says it's important for everybody to try and remember—